A PLANET IN PERIL

KW-221-714

OUT OF THE BULLDOZER

DISCARDED

60000521877

BookLife
PUBLISHING

All rights reserved.
Printed in Poland.

A catalogue record for this book is available from the British Library.

ISBN: 978-1-80155-889-1

Written by:
Robin Twiddy

Edited by:
William Anthony

Designed by:
Drue Rintoul

©2023
BookLife Publishing Ltd.
King's Lynn, Norfolk
PE30 4LS, UK

All facts, statistics, web addresses and URLs in this book were verified as valid and accurate at time of writing. No responsibility for any changes to external websites or references can be accepted by either the author or publisher.

AN INTRODUCTION TO BOOKLIFE RAPID READERS...

Packed full of gripping topics and twisted tales, BookLife Rapid Readers are perfect for older children looking to propel their reading up to top speed. With three levels based on our planet's fastest animals, children will be able to find the perfect point from which to accelerate their reading journey. From the spooky to the silly, these roaring reads will turn every child at every reading level into a prolific page-turner!

CHEETAH

The fastest animals on land, cheetahs will be taking their first strides as they race to top speed.

MARLIN

The fastest animals under water, marlins will be blasting through their journey.

FALCON

The fastest animals in the air, falcons will be flying at top speed as they tear through the skies.

Photo Credits
All images are courtesy of Shutterstock.com, unless otherwis...
Front Cover – calvindexter, Mykola Mazuryk, Loco...
mimagephotography, Monkey Business Images, Volo...
fotorince, Volodymyr Baleha, Roengrit Kongmuang, ...
rtem. 12–13 – KiKinKing, Oriole Gin, Zoltan Acs, Marc...
Vera Larina, Massimo Dallaglio, Michal Zduniak, sdec...
Satakorn, Alexandros Michailidis. 18–19 – domnitsky...
20–21 – Sergey Kamshylin, philip openshaw, PRESSLA...
24–25 – meunierd, Kuitka Fabian, kpixel, Liz Kcer, we...
Volodymyr Baleha, AVN Photo Lab, polya_olya. 28–29...
Words. 30 – Volodymyr Baleha, Volodymyr Baleha.

WEST NORTHAMPTONSHIRE COUNCIL

60000521877	
Askews & Holts	
BT	

CONTENTS

WORDS THAT LOOK LIKE THIS ARE EXPLAINED IN THE GLOSSARY ON PAGE 31.

BUNKER BLISS

My name is Shona Kowalski and I am 12. I wasn't born when it rained nuclear waste over the UK. Mum and Dad said it sucked.

That's me.

WOW!

I live in this bunker with Mum, Dad and Cunninghams. They are the nicest people I have ever met. Actually, they are the only people I have ever met.

This is Mrs Cunningham. She taught me to read and write.

Dad told me things were very different before the strange rain came. It wasn't really rain. It was nuclear waste.

Dad is the best. He taught me about loads of stuff about the before times.

Mum tried to explain what the sky was, but it didn't really make sense to me. She said to imagine that there wasn't a ceiling.

She showed me this picture but all I can see is blue.

THE BEFORE TIMES

I have learnt a lot about the before times. People used to go for walks, buy things, watch TV and have friends.

OOL-CUT DEN
GET LIT AND STUN YOUR FAM WITH THESE SAVAGE CUTS!

I think I would like some friends my age.

Mr Cunningham was a very good boy wizard.

Every Thursday, the Cunninghams put on a play for me. This week it is Gary Rotter and Warm Cup of Bovril™.

This winter snuggle down in front of a
Nambie Fire Place

Mum said that a lot of the things people used to do used a lot of power, such as watching TV. This power was made by burning <u>fossil fuels</u>.

Mum said that this fire burned coal. This is a type of fossil fuel.

I tried to learn as much as I could about the before times. A lot of what I know comes from these magazines that I found in the bunker.

A GOVERNMENT MAN

Dad worked for the government in the before times. He said that fossil fuels had become a big problem. They were killing the planet and people needed to find an <u>alternative</u>.

This is Dad in the before times. I think that is more sky behind him.

Making electricity with fossil fuels was releasing something called <u>carbon dioxide</u>. It was making the world hotter. He said it would cause lots of floods and heatwaves. It was Dad's job to find an alternative.

Dad had to look at all the different options for powering the country and pick one. He said there were really only three options.

Wind power

Solar power

Nuclear power

Dad wanted to use wind and solar power. The bigwigs didn't want to spend the money on two types of technology. I think he still feels guilty about picking nuclear power.

WHY NUCLEAR?

I found some of Dad's notes. They make it sound like nuclear power wasn't so bad. He wrote...

... Nuclear reactors have been in use since the 1960s. In the 60 years that they have been used, there have only been three major accidents.

Dad seemed pretty on board at this point.

Some of Dad's notes were about carbon footprints. These are a way of saying how much carbon pollution something makes. His notes say that nuclear power plants have a carbon footprint of zero.

Dad said the carbon footprint thing wasn't really true. A lot of carbon is made when they build and dismantle them.

His nasty boss made him write that.

THE WRONG SOLUTION

The government chose nuclear power. It didn't take long before all the old coal and oil plants had been replaced with nuclear power plants.

THE UK WELCOMES A FUTURE OF CLEAN, RENEWABLE NUCLEAR POWER.

Some people were scared that there would be another nuclear meltdown like the one at Chernobyl. I found some old pictures of Chernobyl. It looks really spooky. I wonder if the world looks like that outside.

CHERNOBYL: EVACUATED FOR 30 KILOMETRES AFTER DISASTER AT NUCLEAR PLANT.

Well, everything was fine except for the obvious problem. Nuclear power plants make nuclear waste. Nuclear waste is bad! The government had to come up with a way to get rid of it safely.

WHY

Some countries were burying the waste in concrete. That just made problems for the future. That is when someone had the bright idea of firing it into space!

IT'S RAINING WASTE

Mum showed me footage on her old phone of the day the rocket launched. It looked like everyone was watching. People were chanting, "Shoot that waste into space".

Everyone cheered when the rocket launched. It was taking away our big problem. But then it happened. The rocket exploded.

Plutonium and bits of metal rained from the sky. Dad managed to take a few photos of the destruction before rushing Mum to his bunker.

The falling metal destroyed homes and lives. Yet this was only the beginning. Worse than the debris was the nuclear waste that covered the country.

Mrs Cunningham took this picture before she got to the bunker.

Dad explained how nuclear power works. He said it is like having a tank filled with ping pong balls on mouse traps.

If you dropped one ping pong ball in, it would set off a mousetrap and release another ping pong ball. Then another, and so on.

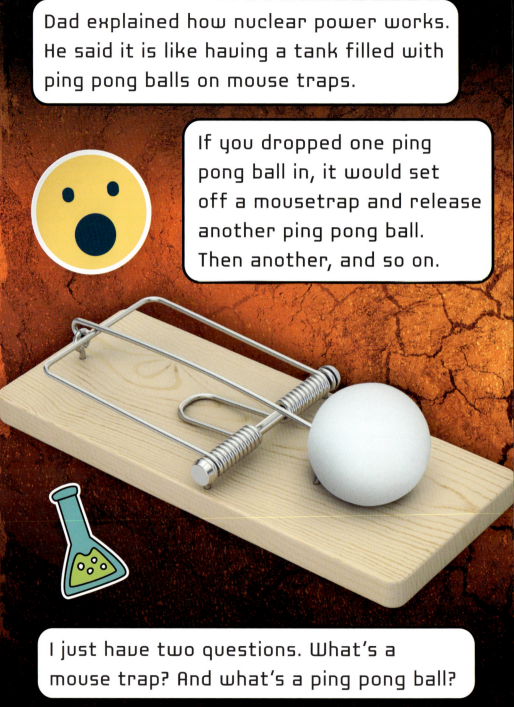

I just have two questions. What's a mouse trap? And what's a ping pong ball?

Once the <u>uranium</u> and plutonium have been used up, they stay very <u>radioactive</u> and dangerous. They give off radiation that affects the <u>cells</u> of living things.

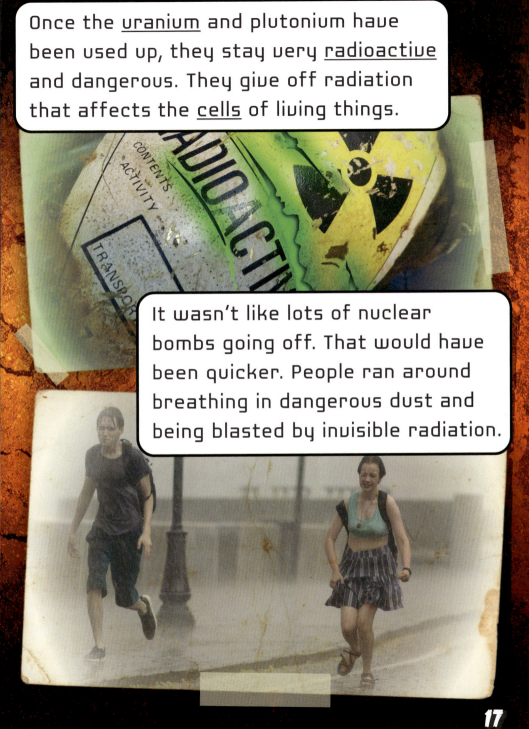

It wasn't like lots of nuclear bombs going off. That would have been quicker. People ran around breathing in dangerous dust and being blasted by invisible radiation.

DAD HAS A PLAN

Dad told us his plan whilst we ate breakfast this morning. We don't have many options for food in the bunker. My favourite is baked beans and pickled gherkins.

Dad said that we were running out of food. He also said that he had got hold of someone on the radio. They said that France wasn't affected by the radiation.

Dad said that we would be safe if we could make it to the Channel Tunnel. I started getting my stuff together. Mrs Cunningham said that she was feeling too ill to come with us.

Mr Cunningham said that he would stay with her. Mum and Dad got ready as I said goodbye to Mrs Cunningham.

OUTSIDE AT LAST

Dad gave us these funny suits that he said would protect us from the radiation. He also gave me a Geiger counter. It measures radiation.

The world wasn't as broken as I expected. It was just a bit run down. Dad said most of the damage was done during the riots.

It was weird leaving the bunker for the first time. Now I know what the sky looks like. It's big!

Dad said the real danger was the invisible radiation. He said that we needed to keep checking the Geiger counter to make sure that we weren't walking into more radiation.

Here is me checking some grass with the Geiger counter. Being outside is so much fun.

I hadn't realised how much space there was outside. The wind is very different to my electric fan in the bunker.

Here's Mum checking the radioactivity of a tree.

WHERE ARE THE MUTANTS?

We found a house with people in it. I thought that if we found people, they would be mutants with three arms and giant heads. Yet, they just looked like normal people.

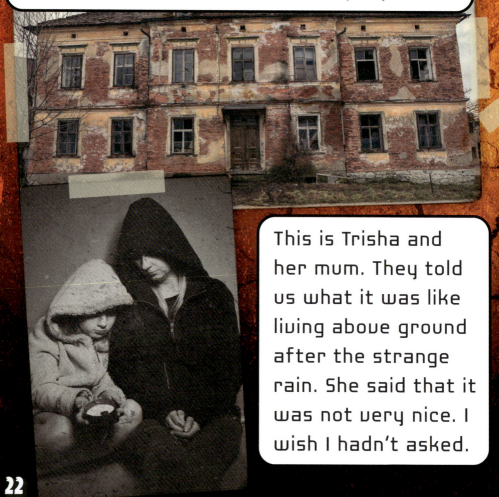

This is Trisha and her mum. They told us what it was like living above ground after the strange rain. She said that it was not very nice. I wish I hadn't asked.

Trisha's mum said that it rained heavily for the first few weeks. She said that the rain was black and oily because of the radioactive soot from the explosion. Yuck!

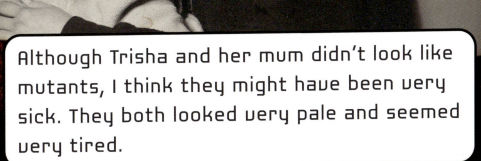

Although Trisha and her mum didn't look like mutants, I think they might have been very sick. They both looked very pale and seemed very tired.

ARE THE PLANTS OK?

We had to leave Trisha and her mum. Mum had checked the Geiger counter and the house was really radioactive. Not good!

There were a lot more bushes, trees and flowers around than I thought. I thought everything would be brown and grey and that all the plants would have died. Yet, there seemed to be vegetation everywhere.

Mum showed me the leaves on the plants, and they weren't quite as normal as they first looked.

Mum had this book. It wouldn't be any good now. The Geiger counter is more helpful.

Mum said courgettes weren't supposed to be that shape and she showed me a picture of what they were supposed to look like. The Geiger counter was going bonkers.

SEARCH FOR SHELTER

It was starting to get dark. We needed to find shelter. Dad said that we should find somewhere that could protect us from the rain. It might still be radioactive.

Dad looking for shelter

Not as nice as the bunker!

Dad found a basement for us to stay in. He said it had thick enough walls to block most of the radiation.

GOOD VIBES

I don't really know much about the world at all, but I am sure it was better than this. I miss Mr and Mrs Cunningham. I hope that they are alright.

Before they went to sleep, Mum and Dad told me stories about their life before the strange rain. They said that I could have normal things such as pets when we get to France.

LEAVING THE WASTELAND

In the morning, we walked for an hour. We had to avoid some heavily radioactive areas. Soon, we were at the Channel Tunnel. We would be safe in France once we got through the tunnel.

Dad said most dogs have four legs.

On the way, we saw a pack of dogs. I really wanted to stroke them. Dad said it wasn't a good idea. He said that their fur was radioactive. But they were so cute!

The tunnel was really creepy. It was very dark. This was the first time the Geiger counter hadn't gone crazy since we left the bunker.

Eventually, we made it to the quarantine zone. The soldiers there tested us to make sure that we were not too radioactive. Some people from the UK had absorbed so much radiation that they were dangerous.

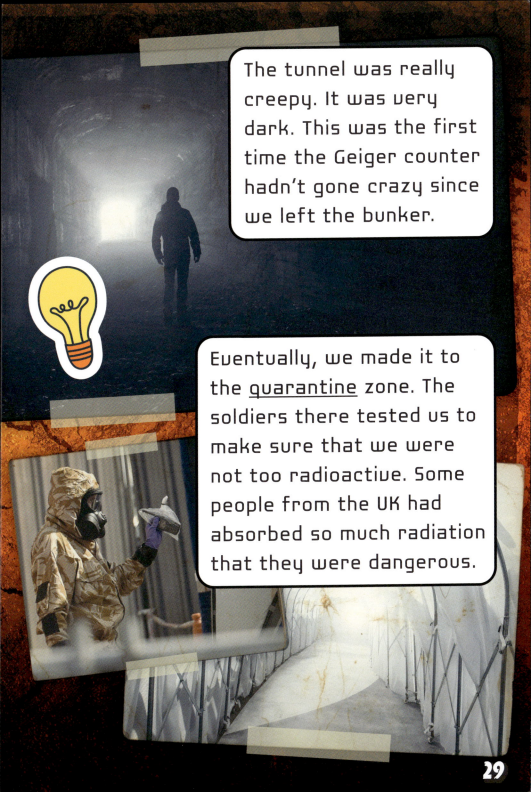

A NUCLEAR-FREE WORLD

I have been living in France for a few months now. Our new house is much nicer than my old bunker and I have made some friends. All nuclear power was banned after the rest of the world saw what happened to the UK.

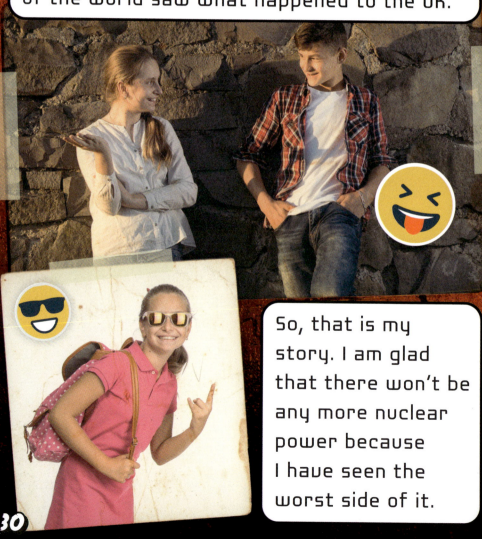

So, that is my story. I am glad that there won't be any more nuclear power because I have seen the worst side of it.

GLOSSARY

ALTERNATIVE   a different option

CARBON DIOXIDE   something that is found in the air that humans breathe out

CELLS   the basic building blocks that make up all living things

CHERNOBYL   a city in Ukraine which was the location of one of the largest nuclear disasters in history

FOSSIL FUELS   things burned to make energy, such as coal, oil and gas, which formed millions of years ago from the remains of animals and plants

NUCLEAR MELTDOWN   an accident in a nuclear reactor caused by the nuclear core melting and releasing radiation

PLUTONIUM   a radioactive material used in producing nuclear energy

QUARANTINE   keeping a person or animal separated from others to stop the spreading of disease or illness

RADIOACTIVE   letting out radiation

URANIUM   a heavy, silver-white radioactive metal

INDEX